# Cassie Pup

## Favorite ladybug and Snake Stories

### (Children's Rhymes For Ages 3-8)

**Sheri Poe-Pape**
*Illustrated By : Harry Aveira*

Cassie Pup's Favorite Ladybug and Snake Stories
(Children's Rhymes for Age 3-8)
Copyright © 2018 Sheri Poe-Pape
Illustrations by Harry Aveira

Publisher's Cataloging-In-Publication Data

Poe-Pape, Sheri
Cassie Pup's Favorite Ladybug and Snake Stories;
by Sheri Poe-Pape;
Illustrated by Harry Aveira

Summary: In this sequel to "Cassie's Marvelous Music Lessons," Cassie Pup hosts her two favorite stories covering Lucy the Loony Ladybug and Clairborne the Cha Cha Cobra. Rhyming and hilarious situations are set in both forest and jungle themes.

Audience: Ages 3-8
ISBN-13: 978-1797051543

1. Dogs-Juvenile fiction.
2. Ladybugs-Juvenile fiction.
3. Snakes-Juvenile fiction.
4. Humorous stories.
5. Stories in rhyme.
6. Dogs-fiction
7. Ladybugs-fiction.
8. Snakes-fiction.

PZ7.1P635Ca 2020          (E)Dc23

Book and Author Information: www.sheripoe-pape.com

Dedicated to Mrs. Connie Mayfield,
my kindergarten teacher; the second person to read to me as a child.

More Cassie Books are on their way!  Be sure to get your copy of *Cassie's Marvelous Music Lessons*, the one that started it all, winner of the Midwest Publishing Association, Story Monsters Approved and Royal Dragonfly Children's Book Awards.  Also get the first sequel, *Cassie Pup Takes the Cake??*, winner of the Purple Dragonfly, Story Monsters Approved, New Apple Literary and Reader's Favorite Children's Book Awards.  Both are also Amazon Bestsellers.

All books available through Barnes and Noble and Amazon.

Join my email list and receive a free coloring page!

www.sheripoe-pape.com

# Lucy
## the Loopy Ladybug?

Lucy the ladybug sat upon a frog log,
in Lilac Forest amidst a pale blue fog.

Her antennae erect, all spots correct,
Miss Lucy started to change color.

From tealy turquoise to all tangerine,
Lucy's skin feeling not so pristine.
Peach to Scotch plaid, a bug gone mad?
What color will Lucy wear next?

Peppermint twist to blue stripes amiss,
Lady Bug at the end of one's rope?

Until along the way, during Lucy's play day,
the lady spotted a cure to cope.

With a swing and sway,
Clem Chameleon did say,

"Good Morning, Miss Bug!"
not a bit shy.

A remarkable creature, fully rainbowed,
ol' Miss Lucy squeaked out such a cry!

11

"Never have viewed the very likes of you,
now your body so green like a dollar.
Reminds me much as the old timers howl
you are truly 'a horse of a different color!'"

Clever Clem replied, "With your crazy design
and my vivid colors galore,

we should roam the forest together,
for the other creatures to adore!"

# Claiborne
## the Cha Cha Cobra

Claiborne Cobra loves to dance,
she will swing and swoosh.
Head and hood erect,
in her favorite grass or bush.

Claiborne is a dancing fool
and "Queen of the Cha Cha Cha."
A most lively Cuban dance;
Claiborne will leave you in awe.

20

21

Practice, practice is her way,
to be the dancing champ.
"One, two, cha cha cha;"
she seems quite the vamp.

Miko Mongoose, dancing king, likes to strut his stuff, you see, hunting snakes is just never enough.

Saturday night at the Tiki Hut Hall,
Claiborne is ready to shine.
With her diamond sombrero
she cleverly dreams,
every dance divine and mine!

Miko dressed in sequined tie,
sets his cap on winning prize.
A year's supply of "Snake Delight,"
delish in every shape, color and size.

Now each contestant, take your place, without a battle or brawl.
Otherwise the necks of you two will result in a knotted ball!

The dance went on, and Claiborne took first.
Miko did well, but lose he would not.
He rose up to show Claiborne who was boss,
but she had cha-cha'd and would never be caught!!

## About the Author

Sheri Poe-Pape has written many internet and newspaper articles about people in the arts and history and has been the Director/Educator of the Pape Conservatory of Music for the past forty years. She is the author of two children's picture books, the Award-winning *Cassie's Marvelous Music Lessons* and *Cassie Pup takes the Cake??* Each day, she warms up on the piano, and for fifteen of those years, a small dog has been her constant companion.

In recent years, little Cassie has stood on the right side of the keyboard and brushed the author's hands off the keys—a habit that inspired the first book! Cassie's love of helping Sheri bake inspired her second book, a sequel, *Cassie's Pup takes the Cake??* The author is a graduate of Northern Illinois University where she studied Music, English, and Creative Writing. She lives with her family in northern Illinois, where she continues to write and to teach music—alongside Cassie.

## About the Illustrator

Harry Aveira has been creating children's books for twenty years with more than a hundred books (and counting). He loves partnering with authors to help bring their stories to life. Harry lives in Indonesia with his two daughters and his wife.

Made in United States
Troutdale, OR
07/03/2024